I0735545

DARK TALES
FROM THE STRANGE WYRLD

THE BOY WHO RAN AWAY

PARAMJIT S. BHARJ

OTHER BOOKS BY THE AUTHOR:

The STRANGE WYRLD Saga

1. THE ELEMENTAL - April 2018
2. Coming Spring 2019

The DARK TALES Series

1. THE JOBSEEKER - July 2018
2. THE BOY WHO RAN AWAY - Aug 2018
3. THE NUMBER-MEN - Coming Nov 2018

DARK TALES
FROM THE STRANGE WYRLD

THE BOY WHO RAN AWAY

PARAMJIT S. BHARJ

WEMBLEY HOUSE
LONDON, ENGLAND

This edition published in 2018 by

WEMBLEY HOUSE
LONDON, ENGLAND

www.wembleyhouse.com
www.bharjauthor.com

Copyright © PARAMJIT S. BHARJ 2018

Paramjit S. Bharj asserts the moral right to be identified as the author of this work in accordance with the Copyright, Designs and Patents Act 1988.

ISBN: 978-1-9999699-6-7
Paperback Edition

1

All rights reserved. No part of this document may be reproduced or transmitted in any form or by any means, electronic, mechanical, photocopying, recording, or otherwise, without prior written permission of Wembley House.

This is a work of fiction. Names, characters, places, and incidents either are the product of the author's imagination or are used fictitiously, and any resemblance to actual persons, living or dead, businesses, companies, events, or locales is entirely coincidental.

THE BOY WHO RAN AWAY
is dedicated to all those who have
sacrificed their lives for racial equality.

Thank you.

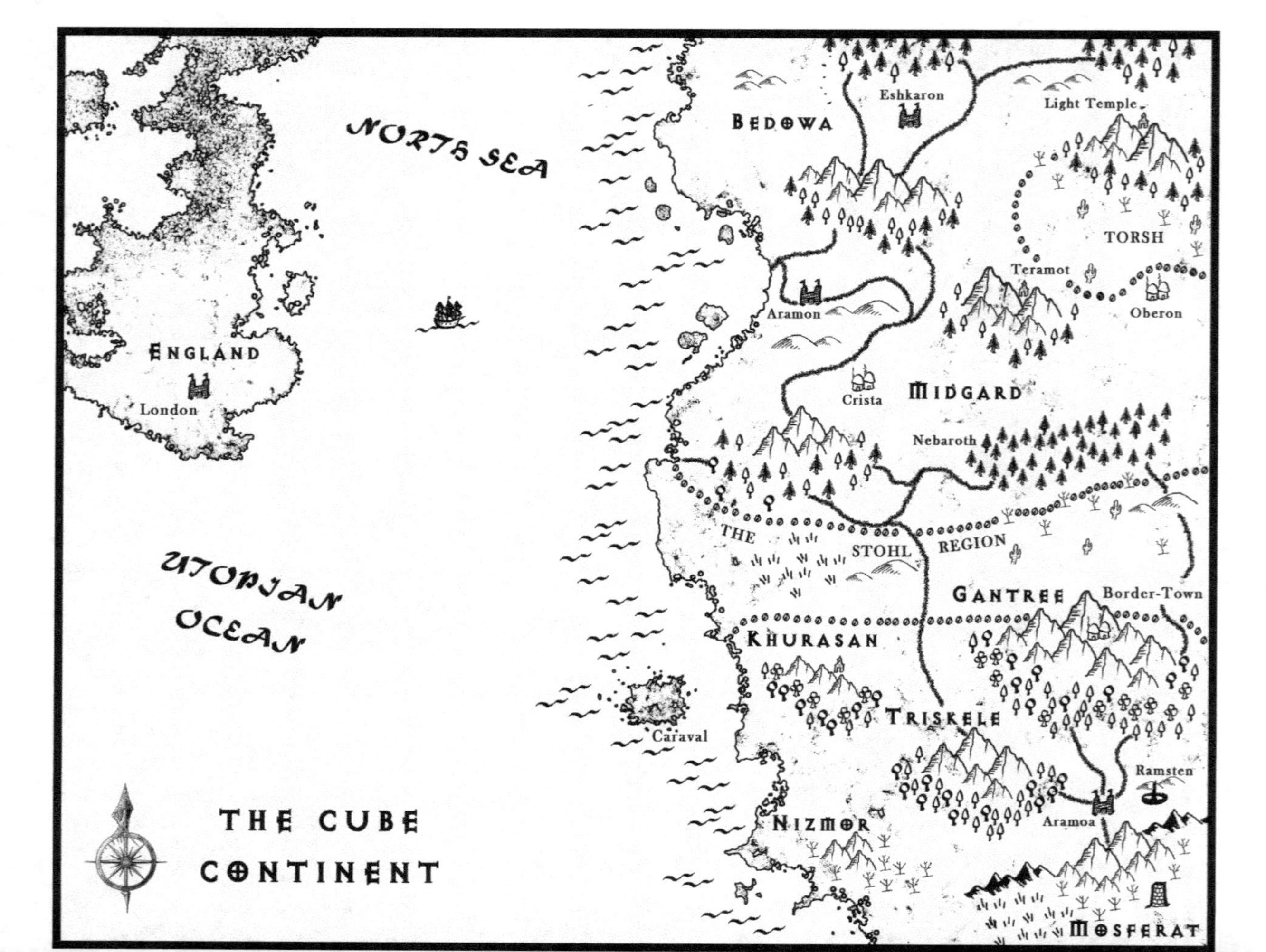

NORTH SEA
ENGLAND
London
UTOPIAN OCEAN
BEDOWA
Eshkaron
Light Temple
TORSH
Teramot
Oberon
Aramon
Crista
MIDGARD
Nebaroth
THE STOHL REGION
GANTREE
Border-Town
KHURASAN
TRISKELE
Caraval
NIZMOR
Aramoa
Ramsten
MOSFERAT
THE CUBE CONTINENT

CONTENTS

ONE

MARTHA'S SON

EARTH, UNITED STATES OF AMERICA, TEXAS, 1874 A.D. (Before Zero Year)

AND THEN it was all over.

A million lives lost in the space of two minutes, obliterated possibilities flushed away forever. He dropped the magazine on the floor and forgot to wash his hands after wiping. The tall thin man of advancing years left the 'shit-house' and made his way carefully onto the stage.

"We shall overcome!" shouted Jeremiah Tanner to the wild cheers of his intoxicated supporters, "We shall overcome!"

"Ours is a righteous war to end the reign of these terrible, terrible people," he continued as he wiped his nose on his sleeve.

Jeremiah was the son of Martha Tanner, infamous for handing over management of her entire plantation to a former slave family. To make matters worse, she had publicly chastised and disowned her only son for sleeping with their women and risking the pollution of her bloodline. No one had seen Martha since her grand speech. Rumour had it that she'd received a telegram, made some last-minute arrangements, then left the state for London, England.

"They're not even people," continued Jeremiah, "They're dawgs, and what do we do with dawgs who don't listen?"

The crowd shouted back many answers, but Jeremiah ignored them all, and hollered, "We shoot them niggers and hang em! Send a message out to the rest of em!"

A short, fat, smug little man named Otis asked, "Er... Jeremiah... do we have to kill them women? You know, they can be mighty..."

Jeremiah laughed.

"Otis, you can keep the women."

Martha Tanner's son recalled his mother's words to her 'employees'.

'You have loved my husband's land and honoured his name and I cannot think of any other way to thank you than to give you what you truly deserve.'

To her only son, she had left nothing. It was really no surprise to Jeremiah for he hadn't done a thing in his rotten life to warrant her love or approval. She was a cold, heartless bitch of a woman but he knew, deep down, that her reasoning was sound - her motives devious. Still, this insult was too much for him to publicly bear, especially with his standing in the Klan.

He had to do something big, and he was about to.

"We'll take back what rightfully belongs to me, and you shall have the pleasure of slaying all those nigger sons of bitches who think they're freemen! They are not, I tell you, and you can kill them all, except for that stain on God's Earth, Earl...and the women -" he winked at Otis "- Earl's mine, and he'll pay a price all right, he'll pay with his life... and his children's too!"

Jeremiah was full of blood lust, with plenty to share with his congregation. He spat out derogatory lines of hatred, fuelled by an intense desire for revenge. The headman of this lynch mob, Jeremiah Tanner, had to appear strong and do away with the black family that lived in his home. Any less would mean banishment from the Klan he held so dear, and embarrassment till the end of his days.

He donned his hood and signalled for his officers, the Hydra, to do the same. Some drunk and others disorderly, the Klan members managed to mount their horses and haphazardly rode out of the abandoned old barn just outside town.

"Let's go burn us some niggers, boys!"

D

TWO

EARL

EARTH, UNITED STATES OF AMERICA, TEXAS, Tanner Plantation, 1874 A.D.

EARL JACKSON stood on the front porch and watched the evening sun set.

Although well built for his age, his body was worn out by years of hard labour. Life on the plantation hadn't always been easy; it meant working from sun up to sun down six days a week and having to eat food that was often not suitable for animals.

The overseers used to be a nasty bunch who resorted to whatever means necessary to get the most work out of the slaves. However, the Boss had died during the war, so his wife took over and conditions seemed to get slightly better, at least for him. Earl had been appointed a Driver to keep control of the other slaves in the plantation, till everything changed.

Soon after that, he was put to work in the plantation house itself, and that's when things really got better and slowed down enough for him to spend a little more time with his family.

What Earl had accomplished in such a short time was unprecedented in these parts and he was sure that not only every white person, but also the other former slaves, looked down on him with spite. Standing alone, he wondered whether there had been another motive behind all the kindness shown to him by Martha Tanner. He used to be the voice of his people, but now, ever since she had forced all this responsibility on him, his family had been living on the edge.

Sure, he'd gained a good position, but his family had become this bright red target and it felt like everyone was ready to take aim and fire. Martha had conveniently left them all alone to fend off the nest of vipers that had surrounded them. He almost wished he'd opened the telegram and read its contents. Martha had burnt the letter after reading it.

Was it a warning? A threat?

Earl recalled that earlier, Lavinia, the maid at the local tavern had been informed by Lester, a cleaner at the local barber that the Klansmen were preparing an attack on the black Tanners. Earl had filed a report with the Sheriff who had done nothing but advise him to go home and lock up or get out of town for the next few days. His exact words had been "Why don't you do like that Martha did and get the hell out of town!"

Must've been a warning.

Earl had borne all of this without losing his composure, but in hindsight he knew that he'd been tempted and played a fool by the devil. He'd put his family directly in harm's way.

Fool! He scolded himself, *Fool to accept that offer.*

On the other hand, he knew that if he had not, it would have been an insult and good ol' Jeremiah would have had to protect his mother's honour.

Damned if I do, and damned if I don't. "DAMN trap if I ever smelt one," he cursed.

If necessary, Earl would send his family away, but then, they wouldn't be safe anywhere without him. Even though the Civil War was over, and all slaves had been declared free men, these were uneasy times and life lines were not as clear cut as they were on paper. Not a violent man, Earl Jackson had decided that the best defence was in numbers. All the local farmers had promised to come and help him today, but no one had turned up.

Numbers, he thought.

Time was running out and Earl knew that they too were concerned about repercussions against their families and their jobs. Either that, or they hated him more than he had thought possible. Earl sighed. It was a heavy one. He looked up and saw the gathering clouds in the sky. They were thick, and he'd be damned if they didn't shoot down hail stones and lighting bolts.

Maybe you might offer me a miracle, he thought. Not for me, but for my boy... my kids.

 He shrugged off such thoughts and straightened his back.

"Man up, Earl!" he told himself.

His family was his responsibility and not the angels. This had to be the night. Earl knew the Klan was desperate to attack. He could feel it in his bones. Rumours had been spreading and the loyal farm hands had spotted increased numbers of strange folk loitering around the boundaries to the property.

Only the farm hands were there to try and put up a good defence. Armed with their pitchforks and axes, they patrolled the front of the house in pairs. This wasn't going to be easy, and it was no time for him to get lost in sentiment.

D

THREE

GIDEON

EARTH, UNITED STATES OF AMERICA, TEXAS, Tanner Main House, 1874 A.D.

THE TANNER Plantation house was magnificent. It had tall white pillars and a beautiful veranda that wrapped around the entire house. It had been in the Tanner family for generations and never had a Negro family fully occupy its hallways. Inside the house, the younger of two children and the only son of Earl and Lucey Jackson, Gideon sat at the kitchen table close to the back door. It was the only door that was not barricaded.

His father had told him, "Son, if things turn sour, and I'm sure they will, then no matter what you see or hear, you get out that back door and you run boy, you run away like you ain't run before." Those were the last words Earl had spoken to him before he'd walked out onto the porch, rifle at the ready.

》 》 》

Gideon stopped playing with his wooden horse and made his way through the creaking corridor to the living room where his mother sat in the lounge with her eleven-year-old daughter Lucinda. Lucey was a tired lady who had suffered badly at the hands of her previous owners. She had a bad knee and was unable to do as much as she used to, which in the Tanner's eyes made her a bad investment.

Lucinda was a mature girl for her age, and her mother had to take extra care of her when she worked around the plantation. At times, Gideon was sent to keep an eye on her, not that her parents didn't trust her. It was the older boys they were afraid of. Lucinda was an attractive young lady who had her mother's high cheek bones and fine form.

Dressed as she is tonight, thought Gideon, *she looks like she's ready to go to heaven.*

Mother and daughter wore matching white dresses and just sat there, holding hands in silent prayer. Gideon was curious about prayer. The seven-year-old had seen so many people pray, and yet those same people had continued to suffer one misfortune after another. Gideon didn't pray anymore, although he did speak to God on occasion. The boy had experienced much suffering in his short life, but none of it would compare to what he was about to face on this, his longest night.

"Mama", asked Gideon, "I don't wanna run... I wanna fight...

with Pa."

Lucey gave the boy a stern look. "You will boy, you will. Just not tonight."

She was proud of Gideon, but this wasn't the time or place to put his hopes up. Lucey knew that something bad was going to happen. She didn't know what, but in these dark days, she knew it would be bad.

"Now don't give me no back talk. Jus' listen to me," her voice was desperate, "and listen well. You run when you must, just like your Pa said. You got that?"

Gideon nodded, then asked, "What about Lucinda? Will she run with me?"

Lucey looked away, wiped her tears then looked Gideon in the eyes.

"Don't worry about your sister," she spoke gently. "She's safe with me... everything will be all right."

The boy knew she was lying. He didn't understand why Lucinda should stay and he should run alone, but he didn't have time to think it over. It was too late.

THE FIRST EXPLOSION threw Earl off his feet as the earth shook all around him. The unwanted guests had arrived.

All he could think about was his family as the second explosion tore through the front of the house. Screaming jeers filled the air. They were everywhere. The riders in white robes charged through the gates and shot the fallen farmers without mercy. Jeremiah Tanner was at the head of this destructive force and rode his horse straight to where Earl was getting to his feet.

BANG!

Earl screamed in agony as he fell back to ground, blood spewing from his leg. The Grand Dragon watched gleefully and dismounted to finish the job.

"Run! Boy… Run!" screamed Earl, as loud as he could.

Using all the strength he had left, Earl scampered away on the ground, when he felt his rifle next to him.

"Lord have mercy," he muttered.

Earl Jackson grabbed the fire arm, cocked the hammer and shot point-blank at Jeremiah Tanner.

The spark lit up Earl's face as the shot tore through the air and the Grand Dragon's neck. Jeremiah Tanner spluttered blood, his puzzled expression unable to comprehend how things had gone so terribly wrong. Earl closed his eyes tight as Jeremiah's blood sprayed all over him - and he never saw them coming. The other Klansmen watched in horror as their Grand Dragon bled out and charged towards his slayer. All earl Jackson could do was watch the impending onslaught.

Gideon, he thought as the first Klansman kicked him in the face.

Before he could even think about anyone else, the others pounced on him, kicking, punching and screaming insults. Then, when he was barely able to move, let alone see, they let loose their furious bullets and shredded the poor man to pieces.

FOUR

THROUGH THE GREEN DOOR

EARTH, UNITED STATES OF AMERICA, TEXAS, Tanner Main House, 1874 A.D.

GIDEON'S EARS were still ringing from the explosion.

The boy couldn't move. Fear held him on the spot as his sister, Lucinda, lay unconscious on the floor amid the rubble. When Lucey saw her boy frozen with fear, she struggled to her feet despite the pain in her knee and dragged Gideon back through the broken corridor and into what was left of the kitchen. Lucey looked him up and down and was relieved to see he was unhurt.

She clasped his little head with both hands and almost broke down. She knew it was time to tell her son what every mother feared, and no mother should have to. Although out of breath, Lucey forced a smile, kissed her son on the cheeks and said, "Run Gideon, run… and don't look back. Don't ever… stop… running."

She hugged him tight to her bosom then pushed him towards the door. Gideon wobbled backwards and wiped his tear-filled eyes. As he opened the kitchen door, he took one last look at his distressed mother. "I love you Mama."

His words crushed Lucey as she watched her only son turn away and do as he was told. He ran, and as he disappeared into the night, poor Lucey crumpled to the floor, terrified at her plight.

Gideon ran off the rear veranda and past the stables where his favourite horse, Midnight, kicked in distress. He ran out into the open fields and then heard the third explosion. It made him stop and look back at the burning house, as it fell to pieces. The smoke of death filled the air and made his eyes sting. Gideon wiped them as his thoughts returned to his family and he repeatedly cried 'Mama, Papa, Lucinda,' as he ran as fast as his little legs would take him.

He was afraid of letting their names go, for they were all he had to hold onto. It was then that he heard horse hooves in the distance. He wasn't moving fast enough. The boy didn't know who, but someone was after him. He had reached the end of the Tanner's Plantation and carefully worked his way through the barb wire fence onto the neighbour's land.

"Ouch!"

He yanked his arm free from the razor-sharp wire.

Gideon's shirt was ripped, and the wire had grazed his arm. He rubbed his arm as he looked around. Gideon knew that he was trespassing, an act punishable by death, but all things considered, it didn't matter. He took a deep breath and was about to run again when he saw a little blue dog with green eyes staring back at him.

Lost for words and afraid this dog was going to attack him, or give away his position, Gideon stepped back. The dog wagged its tail and scampered over to him. It stood on its hind legs and started to lick his arm. Relieved that the dog was friendly, Gideon patted it. Immediately, the dog bolted into the fields, then stopped as if waiting for Gideon to follow. The boy kept his eyes fixed on the dog and ran in its direction. He didn't know why, but it felt like the right thing to do.

At least he's running in the right direction, thought Gideon.

He ran and ran, keeping his eyes fixed on the dog until... he collided face first into something solid.

The force of the impact knocked the wind out of Gideon and sent him falling backwards into the field. He shook his head, then looked up. Unable to focus on the now visibly bright object in front of him, he rubbed his stinging eyes. It was a giant, green wooden door, with strange patterns engraved into it.

That wasn't there... thought Gideon, then started to look for the dog.

It was nowhere to be seen.

Has it gone inside? he pondered, *and besides, what's an old green door doing out here in the middle of this field?*

Dazed and afraid, Gideon got himself up and rubbed his eyes again.

"Am I seeing right?"

He noticed that the door was wedged into a giant moss-covered rock and walked around it.

'A door,' he thought, 'stuck in a rock.'

"Where did you go, boy?" he called out as he glanced around for the dog. "Where did you go?"

He walked back around and mustered up enough courage to touch the bronze door knob. It was cold metal. Gideon stepped back and didn't know what to do. He was caught in a dilemma and looked back towards the burning house in the wee distance, when he heard a soft click. The door was opening.

The boy turned his neck slowly and glimpsed an unfamiliar orange little girl with red eyes watching him from the doorway. Gideon screamed and fell back into the field.

It was too much for him. The sound of horses was getting closer and he didn't know what to do. Gideon tried to hold back his tears but failed. In utter despair, he felt defeated. He wanted his mother and his father, he wanted his sister. He was afraid and had nobody to turn to. He had nothing, and those people... they were coming for him too. Then, he saw the little blue dog standing next to the girl in the doorway.

"W... what do you want?" muttered Gideon as he got back to his feet, when he heard a familiar voice.

"Gideon, please, come inside. It's safe in here. We're all waiting for you," the girl called.

I know that voice.

It was Lucinda's voice, but, this girl wasn't his sister. He'd left her in the house with his mother.

What's going on? "Who... who... are you?" he stammered.

"Gideon, please hurry... they're coming to get you... and your Pa doesn't want that," the girl pleaded.

Pa. That word was the catalyst Gideon needed. *Pa's alive and behind that door.*

He took his first step towards the green door, and then another when the screaming voices made him stop and turn back again. The little girl called out louder, "Gideon, get your ass in here or they're gonna skin you alive!"

Gideon snapped back to attention and sprinted the last five steps before he leapt in to the wide-open door; fear filled his heart as he was swallowed by darkness.

The last thing the boy heard was an older voice shout, "Close the door!"

The orange girl peered out of the dark doorway and as the riders approached, her smile turned sinister. The green door slammed shut, and instantly both the rock and the door vanished into thin air.

Moments later, the Klan riders stormed through the exact spot where the door had stood, searching the fields for the runaway boy.

Unaware of what had actually transpired on this, his longest night, the boy Gideon had run away, farther than he could possibly imagine.

FIVE

IGNATIUS

PUSHPAKA, **Somewhere Out of Time, The Landing Room**

THE OLD man wore spectacles.

The room was so bright that Gideon had to cover his eyes with his hands, but before he did, the first person he'd spotted was the old man with the white beard… and the thin spectacles. As his eyes adjusted, Gideon lowered his hands and noticed that everybody was standing a good distance away from him. There was the old man, the orange girl, the green dog and – this is what really startled him – a moving metal statue that made whirring sounds as it walked towards a table full of buttons and levers.

Gideon clenched his fists and looked back. There was nothing there. The door had disappeared. He swallowed his spit, wiped the tears from his eyes and took a step forward.

"W…w… where am I?" he started.

"A very good question," answered the old man almost immediately.

Gideon wasn't used to compliments from strangers and gulped.

The old man walked up to him and held out his hand.

"My name is Ignatius. Ignatius Voltaire."

Gideon wasn't sure if he should take the man's hand. It was pale and wrinkled with green blue veins spread over it like a net. Still, it would be impolite to refuse and, in his experience, could result in a sound thrashing.

"I… I'm Gideon," said the boy as he shook the old man's hand. "Gideon… Jackson."

"Hello Gideon Jackson," said Ignatius happily.

The old man signalled for the orange girl to come forward. The green dog came first, tail wagging and jumped on Gideon.

"Down Caesar," ordered Ignatius, but the dog wouldn't listen.

"Guess he likes you," smiled the old man, "And anyone Caesar approves of is okay in my book."

Gideon almost smiled when the orange girl came forth and held out her hand.

"I'm Raya," she introduced herself, "I live here."

Ignatius gave her a puzzled look and added, "We all live here."

Raya forced a smile, then asked, "Are you okay, Gideon?"

The boy looked confused and it was clear this was all too much for him to take in at once.

"Good point," said Ignatius. "Let me take him to the garden for some fresh air."

Ignatius was about to lead the boy away, when another, rather well-built, man walked in to the landing room.

"Ah, Nathan," said Ignatius, "So good of you to join us."

"Is this him?" asked Nathan.

Ignatius nodded, "This is the boy… who ran away."

Nathan stared hard at Gideon for a minute, then got down on one knee and looked the boy in the eyes. Nathan reminded Gideon of the postman back on the plantation, except for his moustache. He couldn't help but stare at Nathan's thick black moustache, which curled up on either end.

"Pleased to make your acquaintance," said Nathan in a sharp cockney accent.

Ignatius walked around Nathan and took Gideon by the hand.

"Off we go, young man," he beamed, and led the scared Gideon away through another door, eagerly followed by both the robot and Caesar.

"He's gonna steal your dog," said Nathan to Raya as he stood up.

"No, he's not," grinned the orange girl.

She walked up to Nathan and patted him on the shoulder.

"Like scaring little boys, do you?" she laughed.

"Watch your mouth, Raya," said Nathan. *Immature runt.*

Not even in jest did Nathan Jeshopa tolerate paedophilia. He despised children but hated those who hurt them even more. He was on the edge a little more than usual today. The reason: Ignatius' decision to bring Gideon onboard the Pushpaka. Nathan knew that the boy wasn't supposed to survive the attack on the plantation. As original history had recorded, the boy should have been killed by the Klan members. All eventualities led to it, and now, because of Ignatius' desire to change things and present new eventualities, the boy had lived and all of existence had to pay the price.

Raya sensed Nathan's edginess and immediately regretted her joke. So, she did what she'd learnt to do around temperamental humans. Change the topic.

"What do you think of him?" she asked, "Do you think the boss was right?"

"I bloody hope so," said Nathan. "For all the shit its gonna stir, he better be."

"What's the worst that could happen? He's just a kid."

Nathan gave his student an amused look.

After all these years… "Haven't you learned anything from me?"

"What?" shrugged Raya.

"It's always worse," said Nathan, patting Raya on the shoulder. "Every time the old man decides to break a cosmic law, it's always a lot worse than he lets on."

Raya sighed. "When will I ever get out of this place?"

Nathan knew she was frustrated and wanted to go home and find her relatives.

Raya was Corsan and had been taken from her home-world, Rubidia, over 14 years ago by Ignatius. Her people were being persecuted after a disparate group of Corsans had hacked into the telepathic network and influenced members of the Kildark ruling clan.

The Kildarks were more like the Human species, which meant they held a strong disdain of anyone remotely different to themselves. And the Corsans were very different.

"Better go get your dog back" smiled Nathan, then left Raya alone in the landing room.

D

SIX

THE BOY WHO SHOULDN'T BE

PUSHPAKA, **Somewhere Out of Time, In the Corridors**

GIDEON JACKSON walked with Ignatius along the corridor. There was so much to take in. He looked up at the glass ceiling through which he could see lots of layered multi-coloured clouds and strange birds performing fantastical aerial acrobatics. There were flocks of birds both large and small, some that Gideon swore had scales and others with long feathers that almost looked like Ignatius' beard, only much more interesting. A humongous, unmistakable creature then appeared, which dwarfed everything else.

"What's that?" asked Gideon.

Ignatius looked up. "Oh my…" he muttered, "That's a dragon. Don't want to get too close to that one."

This place was unlike anywhere Gideon had ever been. He pinched himself on the cheek just to make sure it wasn't all a dream.

The things he'd seen since his arrival had both frightened and excited him so much that he'd almost forgotten his predicament. Sadly, as much as he would like that, the little boy couldn't forget his family. The burden of not knowing their fate still weighed heavily on his mind. The closer they got to the garden, the more half-finished and incomplete metal machines Gideon noticed piled up in corners, along with stacks of books, most of which had several different coloured bookmarks in them.

"Unfinished gadgets," explained Voltaire. "Do you like to tinker with things?"

He looked at the boy and muttered, "Probably not."

"Books," started Ignatius, "Now, books are very important, and it is important that you learn to read, and read well."

"I can read some," said Gideon.

"Some… what?" asked Ignatius.

"Words."

"Who taught you these words?"

"Boe," said Gideon, "He taught me and Pa whenever he could."

"Good," smiled Ignatius. "Books are… wyrlds unto themselves."

The old man tapped his forehead. "Knowledge is power, my dear boy, and without it, life isn't worth the effort."

Ignatius picked up a volume entitled 'Sheckler's History of the Technicolour Society."

"This is a good one," he enthused. "I'm mentioned in it quite a lot."

The entire vessel groaned, and Ignatius laughed as he patted the corridor wall and clicked his fingers.

"What was that?" asked Gideon, "And what's this place called?"

"Pushpaka," started Ignatius. "It's a beautiful place, unlike any other."

He coughed to clear his throat.

"You see, Gideon, the Pushpaka more than a time machine. It is a place between time."

Gideon's expression made the old man stop and start again.

"Pushpaka is the name given to this place. It is a large room with many doors."

"Like a mansion?" asked Gideon.

"Precisely," agreed Ignatius, clicking his fingers again.

"Each door can take us to different places, and different times."

The old man had the boy's full attention, so he went on.

"It is a way to go back in time and help your family," then added, "When the time is right."

Gideon's jaw dropped open.

"Why can't we go now?"

Ignatius stopped walking and looked down at the boy.

"You are the reason why, Gideon."

"I don't understand."

"When you are ready to help them, only then can we go back there," said Ignatius, "And not a second before."

"What do you mean?" asked Gideon.

Ignatius examined Gideon's face and smiled.

"You are very important Gideon, not just to me, but to everyone in… this strange wyrld we live in."

"I don't want to be important," said Gideon, "I just want my family back."

"Precisely for that reason, you must do as I say, or I fear you might never get them back."

Gideon looked like he was going to cry but was fighting to hold back his tears.

"Are you following all of this?" quizzed Ignatius.

The boy nodded. He was listening but was secretly wishing he would wake up from this nightmare. As amazing as this place was, it wasn't his home, and he didn't feel safe without his parents near him.

His attention was then taken by the beautiful sandy beaches and bright blue waters he could see through the window on his right. There were fishes with horse heads and curved bodies that were skating across the water's surface and blue people with large black eyes… and fish tails.

"Where is that?" he asked.

Ignatius looked and waved his hands in the air. "That's Orrendorf," he smiled, "A city of Mer-people on the water-world of..."

The old wizard stopped and ran his hand over the window. It rippled like water then Orrendorf faded out of view.

Ignatius realised the boy had been shown something of importance by the Pushpaka but didn't know why. Maybe the water-world had something to do with his future. He wasn't sure, and now wasn't the time to find out.

"I'm not going to lie to you, Gideon," started Ignatius. "There are people out there who want to stop you from succeeding. They want nothing more than to see you and your family suffer and die horribly."

Gideon was lost for words and stared at the old man.

"I am sending you to a very special school," he continued. "It is a place where you will learn all about your new wyrld. You must study very hard, and you must learn... to protect yourself."

Ignatius stopped and tipped his spectacles a little.

"Why are you doing this to me?" asked Gideon. "Can't you just send me back?"

Ignatius sighed and shook his head.

"Why you?" he asked, then answered his own question. "To put it simply, you are the only hope this universe has of surviving the return of the gods."

Gideon's eyes widened as he took a deep breath.

"I know it's a lot to take in," said Ignatius, "But, and there's always a but, you must trust me."

Gideon nodded, which brought a smile to the old wizard's face.

"Good boy. Now, let's go through those doors over there."

"WHAT IS this place?" asked Gideon as they made their way through the garden.

"This is Garden of Peaceful Repose," smiled Ignatius. "It was named so by my predecessor, Tyberian Voltaire."

"Was he your father?" asked Gideon.

"No, no, no," laughed Ignatius, "It's a lot more complicated than that."

"This is one of many gardens in the Pushpaka," continued Ignatius as they walked past multi-coloured bushes unlike any that Gideon had ever seen. There were tall trees with blue and purple leaves and curved branches that linked to other trees. It was as if they were hugging each other, which reminded Gideon of his parents, making him feel a mixture of sad and happy at the same time.

Lots of little animals ran to and fro, as huge white birds flew overhead. They walked on for a bit until they approached a tree covered in pink blossom, under which was set a small table, around which stood two people.

The old wizard nodded to Nathan Jeshopa, who was standing by the table in his beige maintenance overalls and brown leather body warmer.

"Nathan is my chief administrator," said Ignatius. "He runs things around here, although he needs all the help he can get."

"Who's that?" said Gideon, pointing at the droid standing next to Nathan.

"It's rude to point," snapped Ignatius and gently tapped Gideon's hand.

"That…" continued the old wizard as they walked up to the table, "… is HA0-3, pronounced Howie, an android. He's actually a work in progress."

"Nice to see you again," said Nathan.

Gideon sat down next to Ignatius, opposite Nathan, and as the old wizard sat down, Howie picked up a tea pot and asked the boy, "Tea, sir?"

Shocked that the walking statue could speak, Gideon simply nodded.

The droid poured Gideon's cup then moved on to Ignatius. Nathan picked a few sugar cubes from the table, popped one in his mouth, winked at Gideon and flicked the other two in the boy's cup.

"Makes it taste better."

"I think the boy already knows that," said Ignatius to Nathan, then turned his attention to Gideon.

 "Nathan will be escorting you to school and will remain there as your caretaker."

The chief administrator wasn't too pleased with his reassignment but couldn't do anything about it. He knew that the boy's safety was of paramount importance to Ignatius and that he'd been chosen for one reason. Ignatius Voltaire couldn't trust anyone else to do the job.

"We'll be heading out tomorrow," said Nathan, "So, after tea, we will need to get you ship-shape and get your supplies in order."

Nathan turned to Ignatius, "What about Raya's training?"

"I will take it from here. Raya will act as your temporary replacement, until you return."

"That's quite a promotion," said Nathan.

"Isn't she ready?" asked Ignatius.

"Oh, she's ready. I can vouch for her."

"Then that's decided," ended Ignatius.

Gideon raised his hand and asked, "Who else lives here?"

"I'll let Ignatius answer that," said Nathan.

The old wizard put down his cup and dried his moustache with the napkin.

"There were in total around 24 people who once lived here. Now, there are only seven. Howie is the first in a series of new androids designed by Nathan. They will someday, hopefully, fill in the vacant positions onboard the Pushpaka."

"What happened to the others?" asked Gideon.

Ignatius passed the baton to Nathan.

"Pushpaka is an amazing place to live and work," said the chief administrator, "but it's not exactly a paradise. Never has been."

He took a sip of his tea and licked his lips.

"You see, this place is an old God-machine, left alone for unknown reasons. It opens doorways to many places, some good, others not so good."

He looked at Ignatius, and asked, "How am I doing?"

"Spot on," smiled Ignatius, "Spot on."

Nathan continued, "The others got killed when one of the bad doors opened."

Gideon gulped down his tea and placed his cup back on the table, eager to hear more, while the droid distributed some ham and jam sandwiches.

"However, all you've got to know is that Ignatius is here, and everything is going to be all right."

Gideon was relieved to hear that, when the smile vanished from the old wizard's face and he added, "Not quite true. You must make the most of the opportunity you now have before you,"

 "Study hard," he continued, "Learn the ways of this wyrld, and help us save it. This you must do, not just for yourself, but for your entire family."

Ignatius knew the boy had heard enough.

"Now eat up and go with Nathan. He will look after you."

Ignatius Voltaire left Gideon alone with Nathan. He knew Nathan put on a strong front when it came to work with children, but he had a good heart and would steer Gideon in the right direction. The old wizard had much work to do, and possible futures to visit. He only hoped that he hadn't made a mistake with the boy who shouldn't be.

SEVEN

ALONE

PUSHPAKA, **Somewhere Out of Time, The Landing Room**

GIDEON STOOD in the landing room with Raya. He'd been left under her care by the droid, HA0-3.

It was almost time for him to leave the Pushpaka and journey with Nathan to a place called Wembley, where he was going to start school. Gideon wished his mother was here with him. She'd always wanted him to attend a proper school, learn something and be more than just a farmhand. This was Lucey's dream come true, but she wasn't here to enjoy it with Gideon. That hurt.

"What's wrong?" asked Raya.

The boy was frowning and avoiding eye contact, a dead give-away that he was remembering his recent past.

"Nothing," said Gideon.

"Don't lie to me," said Raya, "I can tell, you know."

"Tell what?" asked Gideon.

"When someone isn't telling me the truth."

Gideon sighed.

"I wish my mama was here to see this."

Raya felt bad for the boy and cuddled him.

"I know you do," she said, then paused for a moment, before adding, "So do I."

Raya led Gideon to a small sofa and sat down next to him.

"When I was taken from Rubidia, I also had to leave everyone behind."

"Why?" asked Gideon.

"I was being chased, just like you. The other people, the Kildarks, they were killing all my people. Then, Ignatius showed up and saved me."

"Why couldn't he save your family?"

Raya hesitated, then said, "They were already dead."

Gideon looked at Caesar approach. The dog wagged its tail, then sat across the room in a rocking chair and stared at them with its bright blue eyes.

"I don't know if my family is alive," said Gideon, "I hope they are."

"What did Ignatius promise you?" whispered Raya.

Gideon stared at Caesar and didn't say anything, which made Raya extra suspicious.

"He told me that he would take me home and fix things," she frowned, "Make everything better... bring my family back."

"Can he really do that?" asked Gideon.

"I don't know," said Raya. "This place is magical, and there are so many things I've seen that I wouldn't believe otherwise, but... bringing back the dead? Haven't seen anyone do that before."

Then she turned to look Gideon in the eyes.

"Until I met you."

What?

Gideon's eyes widened.

"What do you mean?"

Raya looked around in case anyone was listening. Only Caesar sat there snoozing away on some mysterious journey of his own.

"You..." started Raya, "You're supposed to be dead."

"No, I'm not," said Gideon. *What's she saying?*

"What I'm gonna tell you is our secret, okay?" asked Raya.

"O... okay," stuttered Gideon, "But..."

"No buts," snapped Raya. "If anyone finds out I told you, I don't know what might happen."

"Okay," said Gideon, "I understand."

No sooner had the two shaken hands when Nathan Jeshopa walked in.

"Glad to see the two of you getting along," he smiled.

Caesar leapt up off the rocking chair and out the door as the tall man sat in the rocking chair.

"Don't worry, Gideon," said Nathan, "You'll see her again."

Gideon and Raya looked at each other and smiled. Then, the orange girl walked up to her teacher.

"Do you need any help with anything?" she asked politely.

"Nope. I'm all packed and so is your young friend," said Nathan. "Got all his gear together in cargo bay 7."

He looked at his watch, then across the room at Gideon.

Why's he staring at me?

"Did she tell you anything interesting..." started Nathan - Raya looked over her shoulder at the boy, afraid they'd been overheard - "...about me?"

"No sir," said Gideon, "Not that you're... not interesting."

Nathan laughed. Gideon's heart skipped a beat, and he was certain Raya's did too.

"It's okay," laughed Nathan. "I know what it feels like. I think we all do... so far away from our homes."

He stood up and walked over to the boy.

"Ready for the rest of your life to start?"

No. No. No.

Gideon looked up at Nathan's most distinguishing feature, his moustache.

"Yes sir," he said as confidently as he could.

Nathan looked at his watch again and sighed. The old man was late, again.

"Raya," he called, "Better go wake Ignatius. He's probably overslept."

The orange girl with the red eyes gave Gideon a smile and then left the landing room. Nathan and the boy stood there waiting for the mastermind to see them off. It was a terrifying moment for Gideon, who was now more confused than ever and wished that Raya hadn't told him anything.

What does she mean? I'm not dead.

Gideon carefully pinched himself. He was most definitely alive.

The boy now knew he wasn't the only one trapped by this place. It seemed that Raya was too, a realisation that brought him strange comfort.

I'm not alone, he thought as he waited for Ignatius Voltaire to send him somewhere he really didn't want to go.

I'm not alone.

EIGHT

THE PROMISE

GAIA, ENG-LAND, HARLESDEN, December 21 1693 A.Z. (After Zero Year) - Two Days Later

THEY EMERGED through a wooden door, having crossed the mists of time and space, at a place known only as the Terminal. There were people everywhere. Gideon watched them all hustling and bustling through tight over-ground corridors. The stench of sweat filled the hot air as the two of them joined the crowd. The Terminal was an old abandoned chemical plant that had been harvested and refitted into a grand central station. It was the main interconnect between the twelve main cities in Eng-land and the trains always ran on schedule. Health and Safety was considered an afterthought, and the preservation of life at the Terminal always came in second place to performance.

Gideon wore a beige raincoat and didn't say much. He was

still in shock and the constant movement from place to place had made him nauseous. Fear filled his eyes as he was dragged along by Nathan, through crowds of strange and frightening people and things he had never seen before.

With his free hand, Nathan Jeshopa felt his rough stubble. Dressed as he was in a black suit and tie, with raincoat to match, Nathan hadn't shaved for days, which made him look rather mean. Quite to the contrary, Gideon felt safer with him than he had with the others, back there in that other place through the hidden doorway.

After they left the Pushpaka, their journey to Wembley hadn't been as straight-forward as they had hoped. Somehow, the two travellers had been tracked and pursued by agents of the Gard, a rogue organisation bent on stealing the Pushpaka from the current Voltaire. This had forced Nathan to contact bounty hunters, assassins and the like - people from another life he'd rather forget - to reach the Terminal in one piece. Nathan knew the presence of the boy had raised their suspicions and wondered if he'd ever have to face-off against them once they discovered just how valuable Gideon really was.

They had arrived from a cold and wet place where Nathan had purchased matching maroon scarves. Gideon's had been irritating him the entire time he'd worn it, so he tried to adjust it.

"Don't remove your scarf," warned Nathan, in his cockney voice as Gideon tugged on it, "...or I might lose you."

Nathan didn't want to bring the boy to this backlot station but had no choice. It was the only terminal with a non-existent border patrol and a direct train to Wembley.

The platform was overcrowded as usual and Nathan had to push and shove his way forward, exchanging a few choice words with a couple of non-compliant people. He dragged Gideon by the collar of his raincoat to the edge of a dirty worn-down platform, where a massive double-decker train arrived slowly on the opposite platform.

Nathan watched the Polarisation Grid Lights. They were still red, which meant the tracks were not safe to cross. He knew that the moment they switched to green, there would be a mad stampede to get across the tracks and onto the platform.

He looked down at Gideon and asked, "How're you doing boy?"

Gideon looked up with wide eyes at the giant man but said nothing.

"All right then", explained Nathan, "When those lights go green, be ready to run. Get onto that platform and wait for me."

Nathan tugged on Gideon's scarf and then his own.

'Good,' he thought, when the lights flashed green.

It was a stampede as Nathan had suspected. Hundreds of passengers leapt off the platform at the same time and fell over each other in a mad rush to get a spot on the train. Nathan had to do something. He pulled out his gun and fired a shot in the air. Like clockwork, everything came to a sudden halt as people screamed and hit the deck for dear life.

"Now!" shouted Nathan as he pulled Gideon onto the tracks next to him. "Run!"

The other passengers realised the shot was a trick to slow them down and stormed forward once more.

As Nathan and Gideon approached the train, the Conductor on the other platform shouted, "Come on, you worthless cunts, get a bloody move on!"

Gideon ran as fast as his little legs would carry him but struggled to keep up with Nathan when he spotted something. It was a woman, and she looked just like... Lucey.

Mama.

 The boy panted for air as he slowed down. Nathan pushed ahead and vanished into the crowd as Gideon changed direction and called out at the top of his voice, "Mama!"

Gideon reached the platform with his eyes fixed on the woman. He hauled himself up and onto the platform and saw the woman dash into the train, when he was accidentally elbowed in the face by another traveller. Gideon fell to the ground.

The boy was knocked about by the other passengers as they crossed paths and collided. They didn't seem to give a damn about anyone else. Gideon did his best to avoid as many boots as possible, and luckily for him, Nathan pushed his way through the crowd and picked him up in time, before a large green man with three layers of fat stomped by.

"What the hell was that about?" shouted Nathan over all the commotion. It was the caretaker's worst nightmare, being in a place full of riotous people all shouting and screaming, trying to kill each other for a seat on the train.

The two of them managed to get onboard. Nathan carried the boy and sat him down on an empty seat.

"I saw her... I saw my Ma!" screamed the boy.

"It's not her," yelled Nathan, holding him close as best he could, but Gideon was determined to find the woman and tried to wriggle out of Nathan's arms.

The caretaker smacked the boy on the cheek.

"Listen, you stupid runt... your mother is dead. She's not here."

Tears welled up in Gideon's eyes as he stared at Nathan, then realising Nathan had loosened his grip, made a dash for it.

"Fuck!" yelled Nathan as Gideon scrambled up a ladder to the upper level and once again tried to find the woman.

Heartbroken and afraid, Gideon's hopes were dashed once more. She was nowhere to be seen. The boy out of time didn't know what to believe anymore. He had seen so much over the last few days that nothing made sense anymore.

Lost and confused, the Gideon looked for a place to hide. He was afraid of what Nathan would do to him, so he squeezed into a tight spot between two passengers' suitcases and settled in. He hated Nathan for hitting him and for telling him his mother was dead. His mother was not dead.

Nathan Jeshopa regretted smacking the boy and climbed halfway up the ladder.

"Gideon," he called out as he searched for the boy.

"Gideon get over here. Let's go."

The boy heard Nathan calling him, but decided to stay put.

Nathan gripped the ladder as the train jerked and threw everyone else off balance.

"Poor signal," muttered Nathan.

The doors were still open, so they weren't going anywhere yet. There was no more space for him on the upper level, so he just stood there on the ladder. He had travelled in far worse conditions before, and from Harlesden it wasn't going to be a long journey to Wembley. If the boy remained on the train, he'd be relatively safe.

The caretaker scanned the seats as best he could when he spotted the boy safely stored between two suitcases. He was relieved. The boy wasn't running anywhere.

Nathan observed the other passengers on the upper level and wished he could shoot the lot of them. Some were talking Football, and others about trivial matters such as what someone had done to someone else and so on. The gossip-mill was ripe on this train and he hated the sounds of so many mouths talking, all at the same time.

Nathan did like football though and tuned in to a conversation just below him about the 'World Cup'. The Football World Cup Finals were to be held at Wembley Stadium over the weekend and due to the last-minute announcement of extra tickets made available to the public, everyone who wanted to be there had travelled in a frenzy to get into or around the stadium. It was Iceland, the current champions, versus the underdogs, West Isles of Gol. Nathan wasn't a fan of either team, but Football was Football. He wished that he could see the game when someone caught his attention. A three-fingered man was watching him from the lower level.

"Magnus."

Nathan recognised the assassin for hire. He was Grillo, a species of genetically mutated humans with scaly skin as hard as rock. Obviously, the Gard had sent him to track Nathan and the boy. The caretaker leapt off the ladder and landed on the deck, taking Magnus by surprise.

"Stop," hollered Magnus as Nathan approached, his gun aimed at the Grillo's head.

"Put your hands where I can see them Magnus," ordered Nathan.

"You bastard," shouted Magnus over the other voices.

Some passengers cowered aside, while the more inquisitive popped open their smart devices and started recording. Others stopped and stared for a split second, but seeing nothing of interest, and without a care, resumed their own conversations.

"Remember what you did to me?" yelled Magnus holding up his disfigured hands.

"Be glad I spared the rest of you," said Nathan, hand on trigger.

Magnus kept his eyes on Nathan's gun.

"Who sent you?" asked Nathan.

"Nobody sent me," lied Magnus. "I'm just here for the football."

Nathan was furious. There were too many cameras pointed at them now, so he couldn't kill Grillo bastard on the spot, any more than Magnus could try to kill him.

Nathan put his gun away and grabbed Magnus by the collar.

"Careful Human," warned Magnus, but Nathan ignored him and pulled him in close.

"If I remember right," threatened Nathan, "I didn't need a gun the last time I gave you a makeover."

Magnus gulped, and was about to say something when Nathan let him go.

"Get the fuck off this train," warned the caretaker.

Magnus shut up and ducked away out of the carriage. Nathan didn't know if Magnus had taken his advice or had doubled back to the next carriage. Then, another thought sent a shiver up his spine as he scanned the passengers.

Any one of these fuckers could be a spy.

When he was sure that Magnus hadn't doubled back, Nathan hurriedly made his way back to the ladder, and was pleasantly surprised to see the other passengers giving him space. Halfway up, he called out to Gideon once more to come over to him. Again, the boy didn't move.

"Gonna have to do something about your manners," yelled Nathan, as he climbed the remaining steps to the upper deck. The steel train doors beeped shut and the train jerked again as it made ready to disembark. Nathan gave a huge sigh as he pushed past some more passengers and squashed himself down next to Gideon.

"What am I going to do with you?" asked Nathan, twirling his moustache.

Gideon didn't say anything, so Nathan patted the boy on the head.

"Listen," said the caretaker, "I know this ain't easy for you. It ain't easy for me either."

Nathan looked up as a few more passengers climbed up the ladder onto the upper level, then turned his attention back to Gideon.

"There are some things you don't understand right now, and I get that. You must trust me when I tell you, things will get better."

The frightened boy looked up at Nathan and took his hand. He'd been crying. Nathan pulled out a napkin and wiped Gideon's eyes.

"I promise you, boy," said Nathan, "Things will get better... for both of us. They have to."

Nathan hugged the boy as the train started to pick up speed and the two of them sat there, between the suitcases in a carriage filled with people unaware that their futures depended on this man and his ward. Nathan knew their long trek was almost over, and that after four more stops they would reach the place they'd both have to call home.

FIN?

NINE

PROPOSITUM

PUBLISHED IN: 'The Journal of the Technicolour Society of Aramon'

DATE: 1764 A.Z. - January 10

The purpose of this article is multifaceted, which to the casual readers amongst you, means that it has many faces. In the context of this article, it is my way of stating that it will mean different things to different readers. Some of you may hate this text, and yet others amongst you may agree with it, almost as much as I do.

It has been many years since the last great war shook our beautiful lands and the old enemy was vanquished. The world moved on and things, as they always do, changed. It was a case of 'out with the old and in with the new', a universal truth that is sadly always followed by another, which is that history always repeats itself.

The vicious tongue of judgement, often seen in the youth of each generation, is used by them to chastise their elders for supposedly making all the wrong decisions that led to such a disagreeable world, but... and there is always a but, those very same children make almost the very same, if not worse, mistakes when they become the elders, only to then be chastised by their youth. Sadly, life is like that - a vicious scripted cycle of repeated occurrences in which only the actors change, but the roles remain the same.

The world environment is a place of infinite possibilities, much like a canvas. Anything is possible here, but what have we done? We have limited ourselves into little boxes of do's and don'ts, can and can't, will and won't. There are so many walls that we have built, within yet more walls, we have cut ourselves off from the realms of infinity and lost touch with reality. The people of this world need to ask themselves the question, where are we now, in this moment, in this place?'

Just like a writer without a pen cannot write, a person without a purpose is useless. People have created so many differences that they are as fragmented as a corrupt hard drive. There are many differences, beautiful differences between the many people that live on this rock, and that's not a bad thing. People must open their eyes and their minds and embrace these, for behind each skin, behind each religion or culture, there are people with feelings, desires, needs and wants. We all strive for perfection in our lives in the form of conditions that foster happiness, contentment, security and plenty. We all want to be happy, to enjoy our time on this plane of existence and create an environment that expands our spiritual growth to prepare us for what comes next, whatever that is.

Our common purpose must be peace and love, concepts that sound flowery, yet contain the foundations for a better world. The Regents of our lands have, for too long, engaged in policies that encourage competition, greed and have turned us into a consumer society. We have become the very parasites that we seek to eradicate. We consume everything on our world, its resources, its purity, its beauty and its innocence. We have become desire-led parasitic beings that will, in the end, be our own undoing.

Fear is the fuel that stops change, and fear is the weapon that is used in all ways to keep the people of this world locked in chains. The Regent of Aramon recently disbanded the Old Council and thus far has made no attempt to replace it with a new 'impartial' opposition party. This is just one example of how far we have diverted from the common purpose.

The people are so afraid of speaking out, that despite

disagreeing with the Regent, no one has thus far spoken against his blatant breach of his forefather's laws. It is my belief in all things good that calls for all the citizens of Aramon, and of all the other cities in Midgard to wake up and take a closer look at what is really going on in Aramon. The Regent has employed many writers, 'word-weavers', to use the power of scripted writing to misinform you.

Word-weavers are an extremely dangerous people. They can put together such ideas that can linger and fester in the mind, and that itself can cause all sorts of trouble. And yet I cannot speak against all of them, for there are some who write beautifully, much needed, pieces that inspire us to transform into something better - just like a butterfly manifests out of chrysalis.

The literary landscape is a beautiful liquid tapestry, fluid in motion, whose purity must remain unbiased and tell the story of our people as it is, and not the way the Regents wants it to be told. All forms of propaganda are destructive, and always get undone in the end.

I include in this article an excerpt from Who Am I? a beautiful piece by Boldark Grey, who looked deep into the human condition and called for all beings to realise their inherent beauty and work with it.

We are all guilty of causing too many ripples in our mind pools and must find a way to let these ripples settle. By doing so, we can clearly see through the surface of our mind pools and witness the smiling Source that is always present there, on the other side, swimming in a sea of stars and having butterfly dreams.

G.V.

'Who am I, but Divinity... lost in tragedy.

In the Source's eyes, I am perfect.

It wrote my part, and in this play,

Causes me to act in a curious way.

Divine mystery, forever undiscovered,

Beyond the snares of science,

Revealing only what we need to know.

In Its will I reside and play my part.

It is the Doer, the Actor and Director.

Without the Source, all ceases to be,

For It truly is the only Reality.'

www.ingramcontent.com/pod-product-compliance
Lightning Source LLC
Chambersburg PA
CBHW071951190726
48293CB00004B/1436